GOLDEN SOUND STORY™

Goldilocks
and the Three Bears

A GOLDEN BOOK • NEW YORK
Western Publishing Company, Inc., Racine, Wisconsin 53404

Adapted by: Ronald Kidd
Illustrated by: Mary Grace Eubank

Once upon a time, in a cottage at the edge of the woods,

there lived a Papa, a Mama, and a Baby **BEAR.**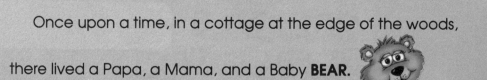

One morning, while waiting for their breakfast to cool, the

BEARS set out for a short walk.

While they were out, a hungry little girl named Goldilocks

wandered into the cottage. In the kitchen she spied three steaming

cereal bowls. She slurped from the biggest bowl of

PORRIDGE. It was too hot.

Then she slurped from the middle-size bowl of

PORRIDGE.  It was too cold. At last she slurped

from the little bowl of **PORRIDGE.** It was just right, so

Goldilocks ate every drop.

Next Goldilocks walked into the parlor to find a place to sit. She

sat in a big rocking **CHAIR,** but it was too hard. Then she

sat in a medium-size rocking **CHAIR,** but it was too soft.

Finally, she sat in the little rocking **CHAIR.** It was just right. Goldilocks rocked back and forth in the **CHAIR,** until suddenly it broke, and she plopped onto the floor.

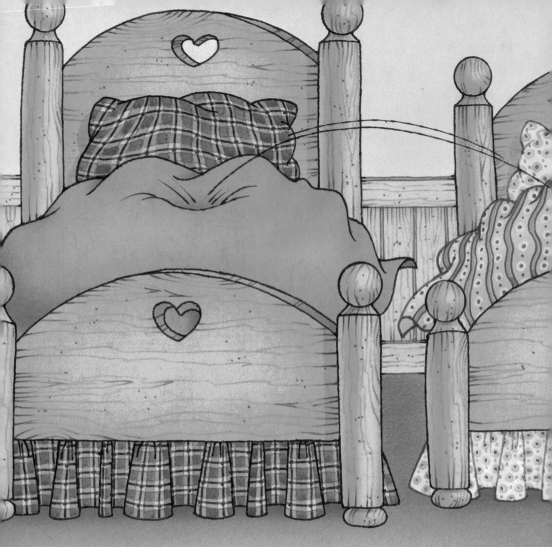

Now, a tired Goldilocks looked for a place to sleep. At the top of

the stairs she found a cozy room. She ran in and bounced on the

biggest **BED.** It was too springy. Then she bounced on

the middle-size **BED,** but it wasn't springy enough.

Finally, she bounced on the little **BED.** It was just right.

So Goldilocks climbed under the covers and closed her eyes.

While Goldilocks was sleeping, in walked the three

BEARS.

"Someone's been eating my **PORRIDGE!**"

exclaimed Papa as he slurped from his bowl.

"Someone's been eating my **PORRIDGE,**"

cried Mama as she licked her spoon.

Baby looked sadly into his empty bowl and squeaked,

"Someone's been eating mine too, and it's all gone."

Next, they went to the parlor. Papa sat down and said,

"Someone's been rocking in my **CHAIR!**"

Then Mama fixed her cushion and grumbled, "Someone's

been rocking in my **CHAIR!**"

Baby pointed sadly to a pile of wood in the middle of the floor.

"Someone's been rocking in mine too, and now it's broken!" he

whined.

The **BEARS**  ran up to the bedroom. Papa tested his mattress and said, "Someone's been sleeping in my **BED!**"

Then Mama tested her mattress and shouted, "Someone's been sleeping in my **BED!**"

Suddenly, there was a rustling noise and Baby cried, "Someone's been sleeping in mine too, and here she is!"

Just then, Goldilocks woke up and saw three faces staring down at her. There stood Papa, Mama, and Baby **BEAR.**

Goldilocks scrambled to her feet. She jumped from the little

BED  to the middle-size **BED,** to

the big **BED.** Then she hurried downstairs.

As she ran through the parlor, Goldilocks bumped into the

biggest **CHAIR.** Then she pushed the middle-size

CHAIR and jumped over the broken rocker.

The **BEARS**  stared in amazement.

As Goldilocks ran through the kitchen, she saw that the biggest

bowl of cereal had stopped steaming. "I bet that's just right," she

thought. Then she gulped down the **PORRIDGE.**

And with that, she ran into the woods never to be seen

again by Papa, Mama, or Baby **BEAR.** And it was

probably just as well.

PUSS IN BOOTS

By Charles Perrault
Adapted by Eric Suben
Illustrated by Lucinda McQueen

A GOLDEN BOOK • NEW YORK
Western Publishing Company, Inc., Racine, Wisconsin 53404

Once there was a poor miller who had three children. When the time came to divide his wealth among them, he had nothing to give but a mill, a donkey, and a cat. The eldest child got the mill, the second child got the donkey, and the youngest child got the cat.

"What good is a cat?" the youngest moaned. "With nothing more than this, I am sure to die of hunger!"

Puss heard these words. "Don't worry, master," he said. "Just give me a sack and a pair of boots, and you will see that things are not so bad as you think."

The master knew that Puss was clever, for he had seen the cat's wonderful ways of catching rats and mice. So he thought the cat might really be able to help him.

When Puss had the things he had asked for, he put on the boots and slung the sack over his shoulder.

He went along till he came to a thicket that was full of rabbits. He put some greens in his sack, then lay still and waited. Soon one of the rabbits sniffed the sack and hopped inside.

Puss quickly pulled the sack shut.

He went to the palace and asked to speak to the king. "Here, sire," he said, "is a rabbit that the Marquis of Carabas asked me to present to you."

"Tell your master," replied the king, "that I thank him."

The next day Puss hid in a wheat field and held his sack open. He caught two partridges and went to present them to the king. The king received the partridges with pleasure.

Every day for the next few months Puss brought the king some small game for his supper.

One day, when he was at the palace, Puss learned that the king was going for a drive along the river with his daughter, the most beautiful princess in the world.

Puss ran home and said to his master, "If you follow my advice, your fortune will be made: You must bathe in the river at the place that I show you. Then let me do what I will."

The master did what the cat advised him, though he didn't know what good might come of it.

While the young man was bathing, the king and his daughter happened to pass by. Puss began to cry with all his might, "Help, help! The Marquis of Carabas is drowning!"

When he heard this cry, the king looked out of the carriage. After recognizing the cat who had brought him so much tasty game, he ordered his guards to go quickly to the aid of the Marquis of Carabas.

Meanwhile, Puss told the king that some robbers had stolen his master's fine clothes and thrown the young man into the river. But really Puss himself had hidden his master's rags under a rock.

The king at once ordered the guards to fetch one of his handsomest suits from the palace.

Puss's master was a good-looking youth. When the beautiful princess saw how fine he looked in her father's rich clothes, she instantly fell in love with him.

The king asked the marquis to step into the carriage and ride with them.

Puss, delighted that his plan was beginning to succeed, ran on ahead. When he came upon some peasants who were harvesting wheat, he said, "Good harvesters, tell the king that this wheat belongs to the Marquis of Carabas, or you will all be punished severely."

Sure enough, when the king passed, he asked the harvesters, "Whose field is this?"

"It belongs to the Marquis of Carabas," they all said together.

"You have fine fields here, Marquis," said the king.

Puss kept running ahead of the carriage. Wherever he saw people working in the fields, he made the same threat. And wherever the king stopped to ask the name of the landlord, he heard the same answer.

"I never knew of anyone who owned as much fine farmland as you," the king told the marquis.

Now, all that fine farmland really belonged to a rich ogre. Puss was careful to find out about the ogre and the things he did.

Puss finally arrived at the ogre's handsome castle and demanded to speak to the owner.

The ogre received Puss as politely as an ogre could
and asked him to sit down.

"They tell me," said Puss, "that you are able to
change yourself into any big animal—for example, a
lion or an elephant."

"That is true," the ogre said. "And to prove it to you,
I will become a lion."

Puss was so frightened to see a lion before him that he raced up the wall and clung to the rafters.

When the ogre had returned to his original form, Puss came down and spoke again.

"They tell me, too," said Puss, "that you are able to take the form of the smallest animal—for example, a rat or a mouse. I cannot believe that!"

"You will see," replied the ogre. And he changed himself into a mouse that scurried across the floor.

Before another moment had passed, Puss pounced and ate the mouse.

Just then Puss heard the king's carriage passing over the castle drawbridge. He ran out and said to the king, "Your Majesty, welcome to the castle of the Marquis of Carabas!"

"What? Marquis!" cried the king. "This handsome castle is yours, too! Let us see inside, if you please."

The marquis offered his hand to the young princess, and they all went inside. There they found a magnificent feast waiting to be eaten. It was the ogre's leftover lunch.

The king was thoroughly pleased with the meal and with the wealthy Marquis of Carabas. He said, "I will have no one but you for my son-in-law."

The marquis, bowing deeply, accepted the honor and married the princess that same day. Puss became a great lord and chased mice only for fun forever after.